Lee Aucoin, *Creative Director*
Jamey Acosta, *Senior Editor*
Heidi Fiedler, *Editor*
Produced and designed by
Denise Ryan & Associates
Illustration © Jane Wallace-Mitchell
Rachelle Cracchiolo, *Publisher*

Teacher Created Materials
5301 Oceanus Drive
Huntington Beach, CA 92649-1030
http://www.tcmpub.com
Paperback: ISBN: 978-1-4333-5638-4
Library Binding: ISBN: 978-1-4807-1737-4

Printed in China
Nordica.072018.CA21800843

SELECTED BY
MICHAEL McMAHON

ILLUSTRATED BY
JANE WALLACE-MITCHELL

Contents

THIS IS JUST TO SAY

If you have feet
I hope
you put on
slippers

when
my spaceship thunderously
shattered
your bedroom window

Forgive me
glass
is unknown
on my home planet

Gail Carson Levine

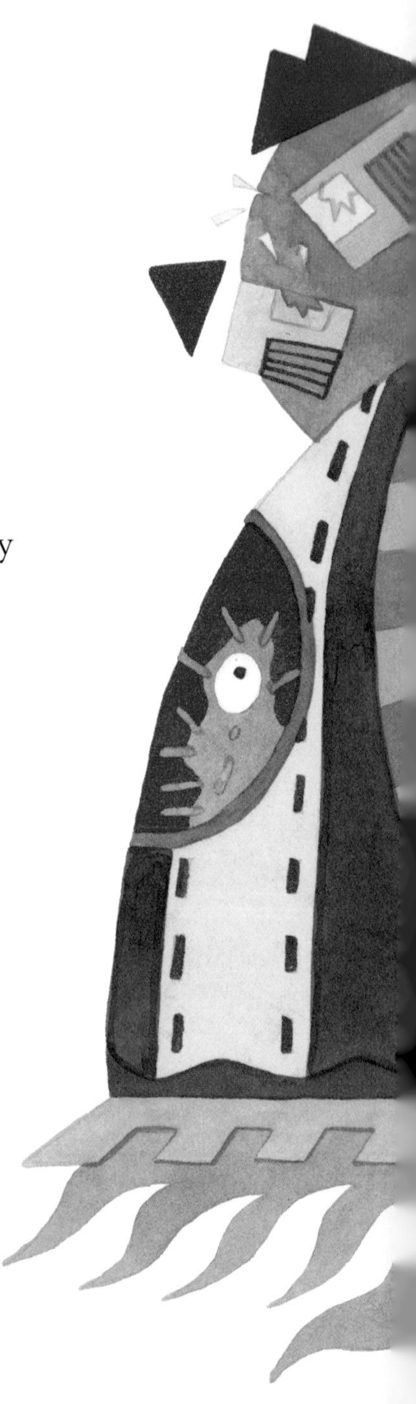

MESSAGE FROM A MOUSE, ASCENDING IN A ROCKET

Attention, architect!
Attention, engineer!
A message from mouse,
Coming clear:

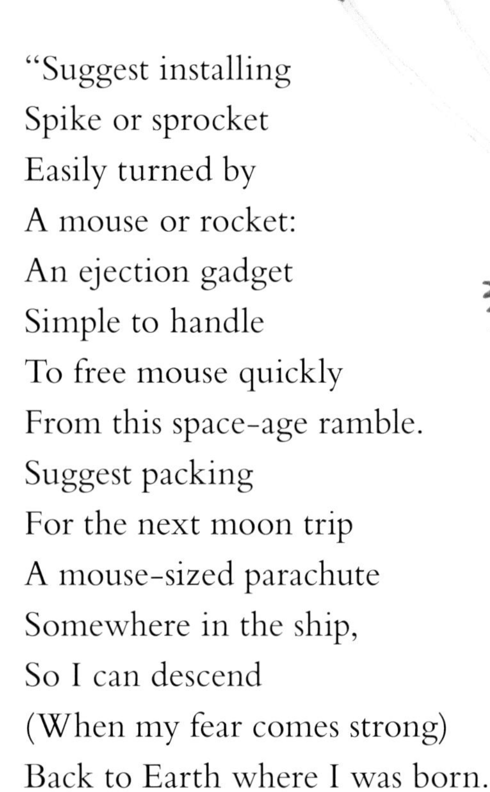

"Suggest installing
Spike or sprocket
Easily turned by
A mouse or rocket:
An ejection gadget
Simple to handle
To free mouse quickly
From this space-age ramble.
Suggest packing
For the next moon trip
A mouse-sized parachute
Somewhere in the ship,
So I can descend
(When my fear comes strong)
Back to Earth where I was born.
Back to the cheerful world of cheese
    And small mice playing,
    And my wife waiting."

Patricia Hubbell

SKY NET

As I went out in the evening
With a sky net that I'd made
I thought it might be useful
To collect meteors that had strayed.

Its net was as fine and silky
And woven strong and light
The mouth was wide and ready
To catch everything in sight.

There were a billion stars a-twinkling
And planets blazing bright
I thought I might just catch some
To save for a cloudy night.

But the stars leaked through the net holes
And the planets moved too fast
So I'll come back out tomorrow
With a fishing line to cast.

R.L. Moore

THE MOON SPEAKS

I, the moon,
would like it known—I
never follow people home. I
simply do not have the time. And
neither do I ever shine. For what you
often see at night is me reflecting solar
light. And I'm not cheese! No, none of
these: no mozzarellas, cheddars, bries, all
you'll find here if you please—are my
dusty, empty seas. And cows do not
jump over me. Now that is simply
lunacy! You used to come and
visit me. Oh, do return,
I'm lonely, see.

James Carter

SPACE ACE

I'm a space ace of skill and daring.
The galaxies ring with my fame
And rows of bright medals I'm wearing.
Darth Vader turns pale at my name.

Superman is my friend and my ally,
And I think him a very nice bloke.
He flies in for supper on Sundays
With a swirl of his colorful cloak.

Fan letters from Venus and Saturn,
And here I'll be quoting a few:
"Dear Sir, I'm your greatest admirer,
Respectfully signed, Doctor Who."

I baffle the shrewdest commanders
And dodge interplanetary trap.
Molecular structures I shatter,
Rogue rockers I ruthlessly zap.

I'm the hero of comet and planet.
My lasers can win any war,
How come that I lose all the battles
With the teacher I have in Grade Four?

Max Fatchen

OUR NEIGHBORS

I met our neighbors from outer space
They looked like us, they had a face,
Arms and teeth and legs and toes,
They wore pleated skirts and fancy clothes;
But they had too many arms and too few feet
And walked on their hands as they went down
    the street.
But they smiled and they said to me, "How da ya do!"
Like everyone does with neighbors who are new;
We became good friends and they are very amused
When I try to shake hands and I still get confused.

R.L. Moore

MISS MELANIE MISH

Here is a picture of Melanie Mish
She hails from the planet of Flong.
She weighs 14 tons and she smells of old fish,
If you think that she's ugly—you're wrong!

For before you, you see the most
beautiful Flonger
The planet of Flong's ever seen.
If you think that she's ugly, you couldn't
be wronger.
Meet Melanie Mish—BEAUTY QUEEN!

Colin McNaughton

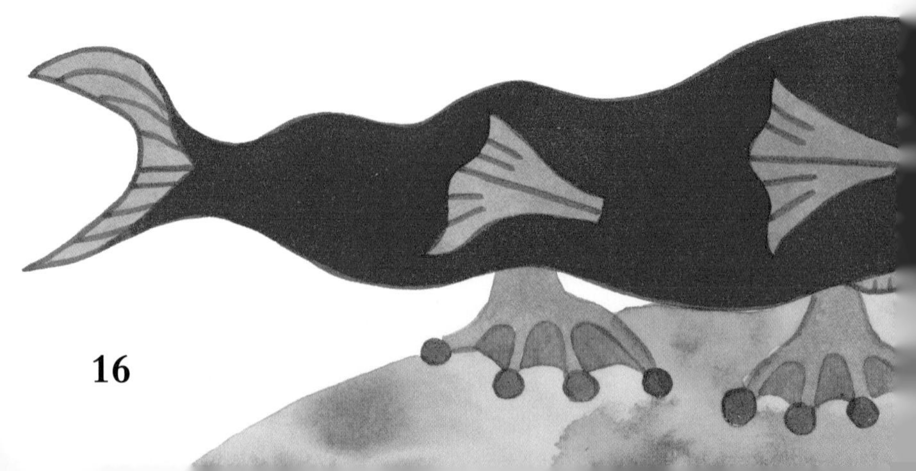

THE MOON IS FULL

The moon is full, you can't get moved.
I'm not going back till it's improved!
It's fit to burst, it's overrun
With aliens in search of fun.

Every crater's jam-packed full;
They say low gravity's the pull.
Those package tours that come from Earth
Make sure they get their money's worth.

Silly T-shirts, solar flares,
Tinted helmets, no one cares!
Hotels as far as the eye can see
Surround the Sea of Tranquillity.

There's no room to swing a cat,
Just souvenirs and tourist tat.
Smaller craters (there are no rules!)
Converted into swimming pools.

I want to know when on vacation,
What is people's motivation?
It baffles me why every race
Should crowd together in one place.

You'd think they'd search for peace and quiet.
It beats me why they never try it.
Alien life forms, cheek by jowl,
The smell of suntan oil is foul!

Fun fairs, drive-ins, fast-food bars,
The stink of duty-free cigars.
I used to come for a month in June,
But that was before the tourist boom.

Next vacation I'll steer clear—
The moon has lost its atmosphere!

Colin McNaughton

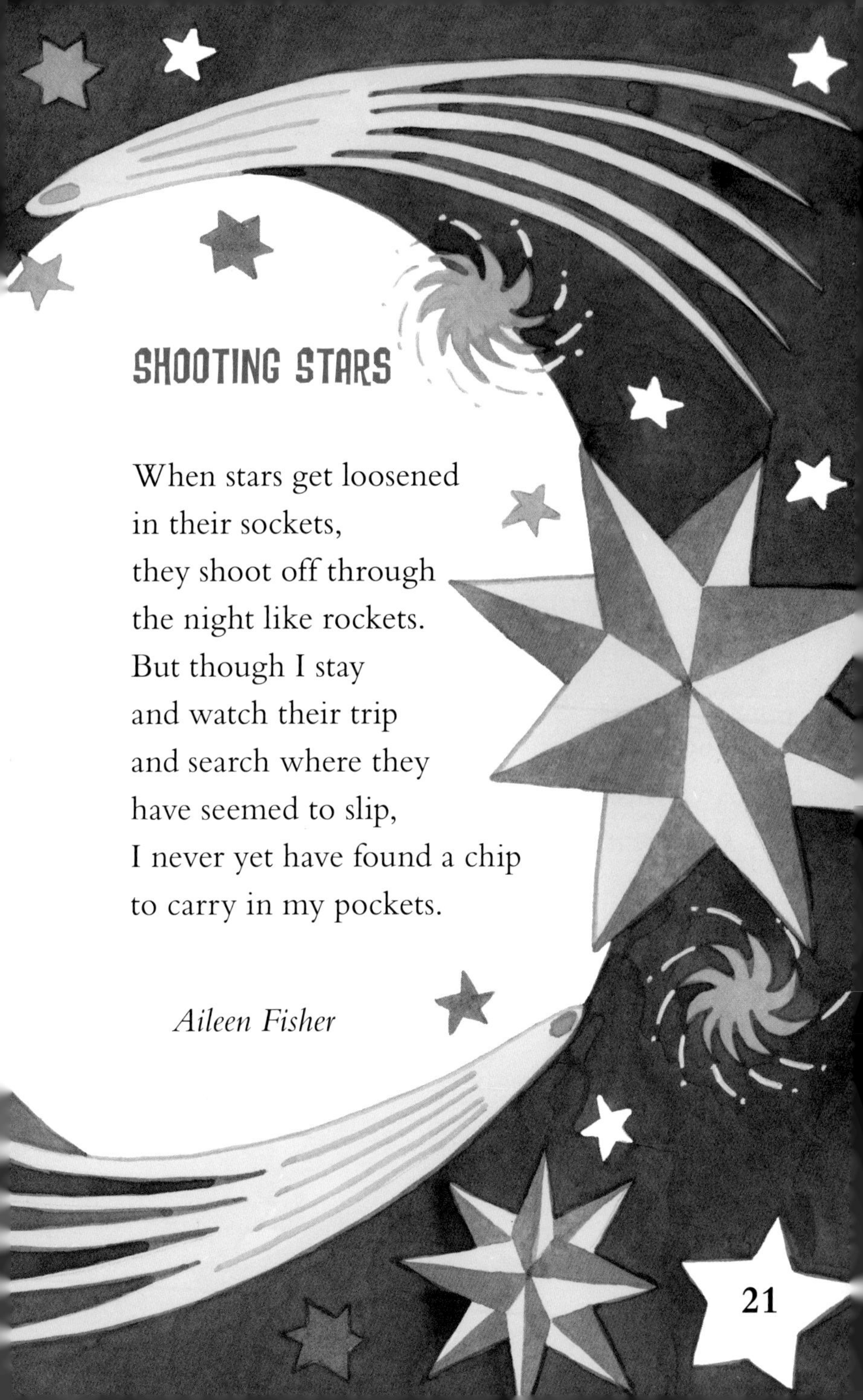

SHOOTING STARS

When stars get loosened
in their sockets,
they shoot off through
the night like rockets.
But though I stay
and watch their trip
and search where they
have seemed to slip,
I never yet have found a chip
to carry in my pockets.

Aileen Fisher

HOW STRANGE IT IS

In the sky
Soft clouds are blowing by,
Nothing more can I see
In the blue air over me.

Yet I know that planetoids and rocket cones,
Telstars studded with blue stones,
And many hundred bits of fins
And other man-made odds and ends
Are wheeling round me out in space
At a breathless astronautic pace.

How strange it is to know
That while I watch the soft clouds blow
So many things I cannot see
Are passing by right over me.

Claudia Lewis

WHAT'S UP THERE?

What's up there?
So far away where comets play
Upwards we stare.
'Way past the moon, can I go there soon?
What's up there?

R.L. Moore

HAPPY LANDING

Oh swifter than the speed of light,
It came from far galactic zones.
Computerized its lonely flight
Past old dead moons and planets' bones.

From hemispheres of gas and dust,
From blazing stars and boiling slime,
It flew, with overpowering thrust
And creatures of another time.

A ball of fire, a sizzling streak.
No interstellar ship was quicker.
It landed in our street this week
And promptly got a parking sticker.

Max Fatchen

NO PARKING

FIRST MOON LANDING

Two highfliers
Buzz and Neil,
Said they couldn't
Wait to feel
Just what kind of
Moon it was—
"Take a look around,"
Said Buzz.

Open the hatch
And out the door,
Down the ladder
To the moonlit floor.
After he had
Sunk his heel
Into the dusty
Ocean, Neil
Knew what a lovely
Moon it was—
"One small step..."
Said Neil to Buzz.

J. Patrick Lewis

LAST LAUGH

They all laughed when I told them
I wanted to be

A woman in space
Floating so free.

But they won't laugh at me
When they finally see
My feet up on Mars
And my face on TV.

Lee Bennett Hopkins

SPACED OUT

She traveled out to Saturn,
A wonderful starry flight.
Her luggage went to Albuquerque...
Why can't they get it right?

R.L. Moore

Sources and Acknowledgments

Carter, James. "The Moon Speaks" from *Greetings, Earthlings! Space Poems.* London: Macmillan Children's Books, 2009. Published by Macmillan Children's Books, London. Reprinted by permission of the author.

Fatchen, Max. "Space Ace" and "Happy Landing" from *A Paddock of Poems.* Adelaide, South Australia: Omnibus Books, Scholastic, 1987.

Fisher, Aileen. "Shooting Stars" from *Blast Off! Poems About Space.* New York: HarperCollins, 1995. Reprinted by permission of HarperCollins, New York.

Hopkins, Lee Bennett. "Last Laugh" from *Blast Off! Poems About Space.* New York: HarperCollins Publishers, 1995. Reprinted by permission of HarperCollins Publishers, New York.

Hubbell, Patricia. "Message from a Mouse, Ascending in a Rocket" from *Catch Me a Wind.* New York: Atheneum Publishers, Simon and Schuster, 1968. Reprinted by permission of Atheneum Publishers, an imprint of Simon and Schuster, New York.

Levine, Gail Carson. "This Is Just to Say" from *Forgive Me, I Meant To Do It: False Apology Poems.* New York: HarperCollins Publishers, 2012. Published by HarperCollins Publishers, New York.

Lewis, Claudia. "How Strange It Is" from *Poems of Earth and Space.* New York: Penguin Group, 1967. Used by permission of Dutton Children's Books, Ltd, a division of Penguin Group, (USA) Inc.

Lewis, J. Patrick. "First Moon Landing" from *Blast Off! Poems About Space.* New York: HarperCollins Publishers, 1995. Reprinted by permission of HarperCollins Publishers, New York.

McNaughton, Colin. "Miss Melanie Mish" from *Wish You Were Here (And I Wasn't).* London: Walker Books, 1999. Reprinted by permission of Walker Books, London. Illustrations not from original publication.

McNaughton, Colin. "The Moon Is Full" from *Who's Been Sleeping in My Porridge?.* Cambridge, MA: Candlewick Press, 1990. Reprinted by permission of Candlewick Press, Cambridge, MA. Illustrations not from original publication.

Moore, R.L. "Our Neighbors," "Sky Net," "Spaced Out," and "What's Up There?" Copyright 2013. Used by permission of the author.